This book belongs to:

_____

A catalogue record for this book is available from the British Library

Published by Ladybird Books Ltd
80 Strand London WC2R 0RL
A Penguin Company

2 4 6 8 10 9 7 5 3 1
© LADYBIRD BOOKS LTD MMVI
LADYBIRD and the device of a Ladybird are trademarks of Ladybird Books Ltd

ISBN-13: 978-1-84646-073-9
ISBN-10: 1-84646-073-5

Printed in Italy

The Gingerbread Man

illustrated by Stephen Holmes

Once upon a time,
a little old woman
made a gingerbread
man. She put him
in the oven to cook.

Soon, the gingerbread
man was cooked. The
little old woman took
him out of the oven.

The gingerbread man
jumped up and ran out
of the door.

"Stop, little gingerbread man!" shouted the little old woman.
"I want to eat you for my tea."

But the gingerbread man would not stop.

The little old woman chased the gingerbread man, but she could not catch him.

11

Soon, the gingerbread man met a cow.

"Stop, little gingerbread man!" shouted the cow. "I want to eat you for my tea."

13

But the gingerbread man would not stop.

The cow chased the gingerbread man, but she could not catch him.

Soon, the gingerbread
man met a horse.

"Stop, little gingerbread
man!" shouted the horse.
"I want to eat you for
my tea."

But the gingerbread man
would not stop.

The horse chased the
gingerbread man, but he
could not catch him.

Soon, the gingerbread man came to a river. There he met a fox.

"I will help you to cross the river," said the fox. "Jump up onto my tail."

So the gingerbread man
jumped onto the fox's tail.

"My feet are wet," said
the gingerbread man.

"Jump up onto my back,"
said the fox.

23

So the gingerbread man
jumped onto the fox's back.

"My feet are still wet,"
said the gingerbread man.

"Jump up onto my head,"
said the fox.

So the gingerbread man jumped onto the fox's head.

Snap! went the fox. And that was the end of the gingerbread man.